prize, Lincoln?

DATE DUE

FE

1978

3 1979

2 1979

About the Book

When Lincoln Farnum guessed the number of gumdrops in the jar at the camera store and won himself a brand-new camera, it really changed his life. It changed his image. It got him in a lot of trouble!

If winning contests was so easy, Lucky Lincoln thought he'd enter dozens and win some great things for the Plum Street Athletic Club clubhouse. Like a color TV . . . a refrigerator for Cokes . . . mitts, footballs. . . .

What Lincoln didn't know was that you don't always win *first* prize — and you *can* get some pretty strange booby prizes. Only Lincoln could have dreamed up a way to use them all — though the result wasn't exactly what he had in mind.

The popular hero of *Who's in Charge of Lincoln?* and *What's New, Lincoln?* is back with all his Plum Street pals and they're zanier and funnier than ever. Somehow Lincoln is always a winner!

About the Author and the Artist

Dale Fife is the author of adult novels, as well as books for boys and girls of all ages. Besides her two other books about Lincoln Farnum, *Who's in Charge of Lincoln?* and *What's New, Lincoln?*, she has written *A Dog Named Dunkel, A Stork for the Bell Tower, Fish in the Castle, The Boy Who Lived in the Railroad Depot, Joe and the Talking Christmas Tree,* and *Walk a Narrow Bridge,* for which she received the 1967 juvenile award of the Martha Kinney Cooper Ohioana Library Association.

Dale Fife's home is San Mateo, California.

Paul Galdone came to the United States from Hungary at the age of fourteen. After studying at the Art Students League in New York, he began his extremely successful career as a children's book illustrator. He has illustrated more than 100 books and has written and adapted several books for which he also did illustrations. He has twice been runner-up for the Caldecott Award.

Paul Galdone lives in Rockland County, New York, where he can enjoy his favorite pastimes, fishing and forestry.

What's the prize

Lincoln?

by DALE FIFE

Illustrated by Paul Galdone

COWARD,McCANN & GEOGHEGAN, INC.
New York

*To Margery Crouch,
and her zest for life.*

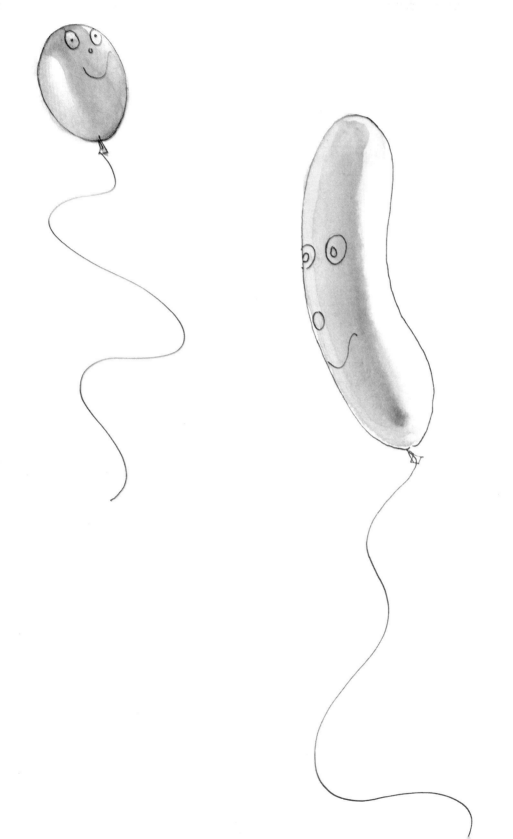

What's the prize, Lincoln?

1

FOR TWO WEEKS NOW, the Plum Street boys and girls had been making wild guesses on the number of gumdrops in the fishbowl in the window of the new camera shop.

All except Lincoln Farnum.

He didn't guess. He studied the problem and came up with the number 7,152,13.

Lincoln arrived at this figure by standing in front of the camera shop window adding, multiplying, subtracting, and dividing into. Figures marched and danced and jangled in his head as he roller skated around the block and played stickball. Even while he ate his meals.

The prize was a camera that took instant finished pictures.

Who won it?

Lincoln, of course.

It changed his image. It changed his life. It got him into a lot of trouble.

When he came charging into the Farnum flat, out of breath, grinning, camera swinging from his shoulder, the family was impressed.

Mom's eyes glowed softly.

Pop grinned. "With Lincoln in the family who needs a computer?" he asked.

Sissy and Sassy, Lincoln's twin sister pests, wanted their pictures taken first thing.

"We've got on our new jumpers," Sissy said.

"We'll be terrific in Kodachrome," Sassy said.

For a sweet moment Lincoln basked in the limelight of his new image. He kept everyone waiting for his decision. "I'll take a family portrait," he condescended. And then he grinned. "As soon as I read how to do it."

Mom took off her smock. Lincoln's big sister, Sara, tied a beaded band around her forehead. Pop pulled Baby Herman out from under the coffee table, and they all trooped outside and stood on the steps and posed as Lincoln told them.

"Say 'cheese,' " he directed.

Everyone did, excepting Baby Herman. He said, *"Goo!"*

Lincoln's first "instant picture" turned out to be a bit lopsided, and the twins were laughing wide enough to show their tonsils; but when Lincoln gave the picture to Mom, she said it was beautiful and she would treasure it forever and ever, and if he would run to the store for a can of cherries, she'd make his favorite pie for supper.

"Zowie!" Lincoln shouted. "Cherry pie!" and he pocketed the coins she gave him.

All this time, Wilbur Green, who lived across the hall from Lincoln, and Bunky Hanson, the little new tagalong kid from down the street, stood watching.

Now Bunky pulled Lincoln's sleeve. "Take our picture," he begged.

"Okay," Lincoln said. "Stand right where you are. Smile."

When it was finished, Wilbur took a look. "It's good of the garbage can," he said.

Bunky's eyes were shining. "It's great, Link. Could I look through the little window?"

"You're too young," Wilbur said. *"Scram."*

"One squint isn't going to hurt the camera," Lincoln said, and he let Bunky look through the viewer.

11

Wilbur turned down Lincoln's offer to have a look. "Too bad the prize wasn't a baseball and bat," he said. "Then we could have some fun."

But Bunky was interested. "How does it work?" he asked.

"Come along and watch," Lincoln said. "I'm going to shoot Plum Street."

They ambled down the street. Lincoln snapped a picture of the city garbage truck grinding away and one of Officer Roberts giving a parking ticket.

"They're neat," Bunky said. "I'll bet the camera store man will put them in his window."

"He puts in just pictures of flowers and pretty scenery," Lincoln said.

Lincoln knew that Bunky was itching to hold the camera, so he handed it to him. "How about your taking one of Wilbur and me?"

Bunky smiled ear to ear as he held the camera carefully and posed them in front of Mr. Luigi's fruit and vegetable market.

When it was finished, all the picture showed was a box of oranges on the sidewalk in front of the store.

"Ha! Ha!" Wilbur laughed. "Some photographer you are."

"You did all right," Lincoln said. "Makes Plum Street look like the tropics."

And then suddenly, as Lincoln looked through the camera viewer, he was a tourist in a far-off place. On safari. That wasn't Fats Butch, Mrs. Patch's wheezy dog, walking along Plum Street. It was a ferocious lion stalking the African veldt. Lincoln wasn't looking at Mrs. Krutznitt's calico cat. It was a dangerous tiger.

Abruptly, three figures stalked menacingly into focus.

Unfriendly tribesmen, Lincoln thought, and then he recognized the swaggering stride of the tall one in the middle, and he landed back on Plum Street fast. The boys coming toward them were from the other end of Plum Street. They belonged to what they called the Stickball Club. The cocky one was Hank Jacks, nicknamed Hands, because his mitts were so big.

"Let's go," Lincoln said, doing a quick about-face.

But the Stickballers caught up.

"It takes a real smart cat to count gumdrops," one of them said.

Lincoln paid no attention.

"Did you read his newspaper?" a second voice asked.

"How *about* that?" a third voice boomed right behind Lincoln, and he knew it belonged to Hands. "Say, Lincoln, where's the athletic club your paper bragged you were starting?"

Lincoln, with the help of Wilbur, Bunky, Sissy, and Sassy, had published a newspaper they called the *Plum Street Informer.* Just one issue had got Lincoln into so much trouble, the newspaper had gone out of business.

"Your paper said anyone on Plum Street could belong to your club," Hands continued. "We've come to join up."

15

"We're not ready yet," Lincoln said over his shoulder.

"Heh! Heh!" Hands jeered. "That's because you haven't got a club."

"We have too. We got a better one than you have," Bunky shouted. "We already had two meetings, and Lincoln's president, and we've got a clubhouse, and furniture and a picture. . . ."

"Show us," Hands demanded, swinging out in front of the three of them, his big hands resting on his hips, a knowing glint in his eye.

They had reached the Farnum steps. A wave of bravado rolled over Lincoln. "We will when we're good and ready," he said.

"*Yeah!*" Wilbur shouted from the top of the stoop.

"Yeah!" Bunky squeaked.

"Okay, King of the Gumdrops," Hands said. "We'll be waiting for that engraved invitation."

Lincoln watched the Stickballers saunter down the street laughing and hooting.

"We told them off, didn't we?" Bunky said.

"We told them," Lincoln said, but he sure wished they hadn't.

Wilbur came down off the stoop. "Just because Hands

16

can shoot baskets easy as flipping marbles into a cup and plays stickball like he made the game up himself, he doesn't have to act like he owns the street."

"He wants to join our club," Bunky said. "You won't let him, will you, Link?"

"Join *what* club? He just wants to show us up. He knows we haven't really got one, and he has. All we've got is Mr. Woods' permission to use the vacant place in back of his drugstore to practice basketball."

"We have too got a clubhouse," Bunky said. His voice dropped to a whisper. "The dugout."

That was the trouble. They had a clubhouse and they didn't have a clubhouse. It was theirs only as long as it was secret. It was really an old abandoned coal cellar under Mr. Woods' drugstore. Mr. Woods didn't even know they had found it. Maybe he didn't know it was there.

The Stickballers had now rounded the corner and were out of sight. But Lincoln knew they would be back. It was time to call a meeting. He gave the secret sign — he wiggled his ears.

Wilbur wiggled his in answer.

Bunky tried, but his ears wouldn't wiggle. His eyebrows went up and down instead.

17

2

THE THREE OF THEM ambled down toward Mr. Woods' drugstore as if they had no particular destination in mind and rounded the corner casually. They walked along the side of the building until they reached a gate set in a high board fence, which they disappeared through after making sure no one was watching.

Now they were in the concreted area behind the drugstore which stringy Mr. Woods, in one of his rare moments of generosity, had said they could use to practice basketball. The square was not very large, and the concrete was humped and cracked, but it was a place. Up until just recently the weather had been either too cold or too rainy to use it. Besides, Uncle Jay, who had promised them a basketball, was still waiting to get it wholesale.

Cautiously they took up their positions.

Wilbur scanned the windows of the apartments all around.

Bunky watched the gate.

Lincoln swiveled his head in all directions. He gave the all-clear whistle, then made for a clump of bushes in the corner alongside the fence. Behind the shrubbery, four secret steps led to a hidden door. Lincoln pushed it open. Wilbur and Bunky were right behind him. Once inside, Lincoln bolted the door.

It took him a moment to get used to the half-light which filtered into the dugout from a narrow window close to the ceiling at street level. The opening had once been the coal chute. A door connected the coal cellar with the main basement under the drugstore, but it was barricaded, the hinges rusted. An empty light socket hung from the ceiling. The furniture consisted of a rickety card table, which Lincoln had salvaged from a trash heap; three cartons, which Wilbur had lugged in from the grocery store to use as chairs; and a sign which Bunky had made and which stood against the soot-blackened cement wall. It read: THE PLUM STREET ATHLETIC CLUB.

Lincoln thought maybe the dugout was the meanest place in town. But it was secret. He loved it. "The meeting will come to order," he said, rapping on the table.

19

Just as they were ready to begin, a pair of heavy shoes walked by the window.

"Maybe it's a spy," Bunky whispered.

"It could be Hands," Wilbur said.

For a moment Lincoln let himself enjoy the scary feeling that the three of them were members of the underground, hiding out from an international villain who looked like Hands.

The shoes paused.

20

Bunky began to shake.

"It's Harry, the mailman," Lincoln said. "Let's get on with the meeting. Will the secretary read the minutes, *please!*"

"I didn't write them down; they're in my head," Wilbur said. "It was decided to furnish the dugout with money received from dues. We figured if we fixed up Mr. Woods' property, he'd let us use it."

"Okay," Lincoln said. "Now we'll have the treasurer's report."

Bunky jingled the coins in his pocket. "It's still fifteen cents."

"Well, we sure can't buy much furniture with that," Wilbur said.

Lincoln folded his arms over his chest. "We'll have to find ways and means to make money. Any suggestions?"

"We could wash cars," Wilbur said.

Lincoln shook his head. "The high schoolers have that sewed up."

Wilbur stretched lazily. "Maybe we could run errands."

"I went to the store yesterday for Mrs. Patch," Bunky said. "She gave me a wormy apple."

"I know a boy who sold seeds," Wilbur said.

"How did he make out?" Lincoln asked.

"Seems not many people around here wanted marigolds. He made fifty cents."

"If we want to impress Mr. Woods, we'll have to think big," Lincoln said.

"I'll bet he doesn't even know this place is here, so how's he going to find out about it?" Wilbur asked.

"When we ask fellows to join our club, that's when," Lincoln said.

"We could keep it just for ourselves," Wilbur said.

"Not anymore we can't," Lincoln said. "Not with the Stickballers on our trail. Hands never gives up once he goes after something."

Wilbur slumped over the table. "Then we're sunk right now."

Suddenly there was a loud pounding on the door.

"Sssh," Lincoln hissed.

They sat so still they could hear footsteps in the drugstore above. Lincoln got a quivery feeling in his stomach, and his skin began to crawl.

Bang! Bang! The pounding was louder now. "Lincoln," a voice shouted. "I know you're in there. *Lincoln,* answer me."

It was Sassy.

Lincoln jumped up and unbolted the door. "Quiet," he said. "How did you find us?"

Sassy pushed her way in. "Easy. I just followed you. Twice."

Now Lincoln was worried. If a girl could track them down, why not Hands?

Sassy looked around. "What a creepy place!"

"No girls allowed in here," Wilbur said.

"Who wants it?" Sassy asked. "I just came because Mom said she's got the crust ready for your pie and to hurry with the cherries or she'll make it rhubarb."

"Okay," Lincoln said, edging her to the door. "And don't tell anyone about this place. It's a secret."

"I know," Sassy said. "Even from Mr. Woods. Wait until he finds out."

"Scram," Lincoln said.

"Scram," Wilbur said.

"Double scram," Bunky said.

Lincoln came back to the table. "Meeting adjourned," he said, pounding his fist. Whereupon the table folded its wobby legs and collapsed to the floor.

3

AT THE MARKET, Lincoln led the way through potato chips, along cakes and cookies, through soft drinks and into the candy lane. They slowed up a bit there, and Bunky jingled the three nickels in his pocket.

"We could buy a candy bar for fifteen cents," Wilbur said.

Bunky stopped jingling and backed away. "It's for furniture," he said.

24

As they moseyed along toward "Canned Goods," they passed the bulletin board, where a gayly colored advertisement caught Lincoln's eye. The picture was of three children sitting on the floor in front of a portable television. Underneath, it read:

TO WIN THIS BEAUTIFUL COLOR TV
ENTER THE HIRAM'S HASH CONTEST.

"That would be a neat prize to win," Wilbur said. "You already won one prize; maybe you can win another."

"How about that!" Lincoln said. "I could put it in the dugout, and that would prove to Mr. Woods that we mean to have a really neat clubhouse."

"It would sure shut up big-time Hands," Wilbur said.

Lincoln tore off an entry blank from the advertisement and read the rules.

"The first thing I have to do is to buy a can of Hiram's Hash so I have a label. Then I have to write a slogan that tells why I like the hash. Let's go find it."

They sprinted around a stack of solid pack tomatoes, through a forest of string beans, to "Hash." Old Hiram's picture was on the hash can, a bearded gent in overalls.

25

"Hash, hash, why do I like hash?" Lincoln asked. "Say, Wilbur, why do you like Old Hiram's Hash?"

Wilbur shrugged.

"Bunky, why do you like it?"

"I never had any," Bunky said. "So how could I say I like it?"

"Well, we'll have to think of a reason," Lincoln said.

"*We?*" Wilbur asked. "You're the one gets A's in stuff like that. Besides, you're lucky."

Say, maybe Wilbur was right. Maybe he was lucky. He didn't have a rabbit's foot, but he did have a dried four-leaf clover he'd found in the park one day. "I think I'll try it," he shouted, can of hash in hand, streaking for the check stand.

"Just one thing," Bunky said, tugging at Lincoln's jacket.

"What's that?" Lincoln asked.

"Your Ma gonna put hash in her cherry pie?"

Without breaking his stride, Lincoln made a U turn, returned the hash, and picked up a can of cherries.

4

Now THAT LINCOLN was aware of contests, he found them advertised everywhere — in magazines, on the radio, TV, newspapers. . . .

There were guessing contests and sweepstakes where you had a lucky number and maybe had already won a thousand dollars. There were contests where you matched donkey ears and contests where you had to find how many bars of soap in a tree. Some contests asked for slogans, and some wanted your opinion in twenty-five words or less.

Now if he could win enough of them, it would solve the problem of fixing up the dugout and making it into a first-class clubhouse. The more he thought about the scheme, the better it seemed. He saw himself winning the color TV, a refrigerator for Cokes, baseballs, mitts, footballs, lounging chairs, et cetera, et cetera, et cetera. Why, when all those things were in the clubhouse, Mr. Woods would be so pleased, he'd let them nail Bunky's sign THE PLUM STREET ATHLETIC CLUB on the fence for all to see.

That would surely stop Hands Jacks in his tracks. There would be no further trouble with him.

There was just one problem. For each entry, Lincoln needed a label or box top.

"What are you doing with all these entry blanks? How are you going to buy this stuff?" Sara asked him one Saturday morning as she whipped through his room with her dust mop and picked up six entry blanks off the floor. Sara was a straightener-upper. If a picture was just a tenth of an inch crooked, her fingers itched to straighten it.

"I'll figure out something," Lincoln said.

And he did.

When his mother was ready to do the big weekend

grocery shopping, he offered to go along and push the cart. In his pocket was his own list.

When they started for the market, Bunky was outside playing with Mrs. Krutznitt's cat. He tagged along.

In the market Lincoln slipped a can of Hiram's Hash into the cart. He had thought up a wonderful slogan: "IF YOU'RE LOW ON CASH, EAT HIRAM'S HASH."

Mrs. Farnum took the can out of the basket and put it back on the shelf. "I make my own hash," she said.

Lincoln took a tube of Magic Shaving Cream off the shelf. Magic wanted his opinion of it in twenty-five words or less. "How about buying this for Pop's birthday?" he suggested.

"Your father's birthday isn't for another six months," Mrs. Farnum said, rejecting the shaving cream.

When they reached "Soaps," Lincoln tried again. He held up a box of Sunshine Washing Powder. "Put a cup of sunshine in your washer to make your clothes whiter, brighter, and lighter," he said.

Mrs. Farnum put a hand to Lincoln's forehead. "You got a fever, son? You're talking funny today."

Lincoln looked at Bunky and shrugged. The cause was hopeless.

When they reached home, Lincoln helped Mom into the house with the groceries, and Bunky disappeared.

Wilbur came over, and he and Lincoln were splitting their sides watching Sissy and Sassy practicing a corny play they had written themselves, when there was a knock on the door and there stood Bunky, holding out a label from a can of Hiram's Hash. "Now you can win the color TV for our clubhouse," he said.

"Great!" Lincoln shouted. "Where did you get it?"

"Mrs. Jones had a can of it she said I could have," Bunky said.

"My slogan's ready," Lincoln said. "All I have to do is put it in an envelope, along with the label."

Bunky dug into his pocket. "I got a Magic Shaving Cream box top, too. I went down the street knocking on doors. Mrs. Ortega's brother uses it."

"*Zowie,*" Lincoln cried. "Now what can I say about Magic Shaving Cream in twenty-five words or less and win us a clock radio?"

"I've got an idea," Sassy said.

Wilbur hooted. "Imagine a girl saying anything in twenty-five words or less. Now give her five hundred. . . ."

"Say, how does this sound?" Lincoln interrupted, "I like Magic Shaving Cream because when I slather it on my face, it feels cool as ice cream."

Sassy giggled. "Top yourself with a cherry and you'll have a Lincoln sundae. Someone will gulp you down and you'll vanish like magic."

"Vanish . . . vanish . . . vanish . . . say I think I can use that word," Lincoln said. "Now listen to this: "I like Magic Shaving Cream because when I use it, *presto,* now you see my beard, now it's vanished."

Sassy put her hands over mouth to strangle her giggles.

Wilbur looked Lincoln in the eye. "You gotta be loco to waste a stamp on that."

Bunky tugged at Lincoln's sleeve. "It's *great,*" he said, eyes shining.

"Thanks, pal," Lincoln said, and sealed the envelope. "Together you and I make a good team."

"Yeah," Wilbur said. "You supply the million-dollar ideas and Bunky scrounges for the labels. What a combination. What does Bunky get out of it?"

"The usual."

"What's that?" Wilbur asked.

"Ten percent of the prize."

"How does he get ten percent of a color TV?" Wilbur asked.

"We'll work it out, won't we, Bunk?" Lincoln said.

"No problem," Bunky said.

And thereafter, Bunky was in charge of the label hunt. Trouble was he brought in just about any kind he could find.

One night, when the Farnums were about finished with supper, there was a knock on the door. Pop went to answer. It was Mrs. Hanson, Bunky's mother. She had fire in her eye when she spied Lincoln. "I'm here about the silly contesting that's going on. My Bunky is running all around the neighborhood, ringing doorbells, bothering people for labels. He's even looking in garbage cans. He took all the labels off the cans in my cupboard. Do you know what I opened for dessert tonight? Sauerkraut. I thought it was going to be peaches."

Sassy began to titter, and Sissy choked on a cookie. Soon everyone, including Mrs. Hanson, was laughing.

Mom poured a cup of coffee for Mrs. Hanson.

Pop passed the sugar to her. "My son, the contester, is looking for the golden goose eggs. I'm a plain frying-egg man myself," he said.

Mom laid down one of her "no fooling" rules. "Lincoln, this is the end of your contesting. Do you hear?"

"I hear," Lincoln said.

He didn't really care that much. He'd already entered enough contests to win everything they needed for the clubhouse. Besides, he was out of envelopes, and it wasn't easy to scrounge enough stamp money, even though the Plum Street Athletic Club had voted to turn over its treasury to the cause.

He went outside, and there sat Bunky on the top step. "Don't look now," Bunky whispered. "But see that character across the street?"

Lincoln stole a glance at a boy about his size lounging against the fire hydrant. "Who is it?"

"I think he's an informer. He's been shadowing me."

"What's he informing about?"

"I figure he's one of Hands' crowd, trying to find out where our clubhouse is."

Lincoln looked the boy over carefully. He did look sort of shifty. Yeah, he really had a mean look on what you could see of his face with his baseball cap pulled down to his eyebrows.

So the Stickballers were closing in.

What would their next move be?

He was afraid to guess.

5

NEWS SPREAD FAST on Plum Street.

Soon almost everyone knew about Lincoln's contest fever.

Every time Officer Roberts saw Lincoln he asked him if he'd won anything yet.

Harry, the postman, began shaking his head as soon as he saw Lincoln waiting hopefully by the mailbox.

Bunky made another sign for the clubhouse. It was bigger than he was. He brought it to Lincoln for a look. Under the words THE PLUM STREET ATHLETIC CLUB, he had drawn a basketball, a football, a baseball and bat, a ping-pong table, a TV, a big desk, and four easy chairs.

"What's all that mean?" Lincoln asked.

"It's the inside of our clubhouse," Bunky said.

"Great!" Lincoln said. "But we haven't got any of those things. All we've got is the promise of a basketball from Uncle Jay."

"We will have when your prizes come," Bunky said confidently.

And then they did.

That very day when the postman came, he had a letter for Lincoln. He handed him the long white envelope, edged in red and blue, and then, grinning, waited for Lincoln to open it.

Lincoln let out a shout that brought Sissy and Sassy from the kitchen, Wilbur from across the hall, and Bunky from the stoop outside. "It's from the Hiram Hash Company," Lincoln said, hypnotized by his first airmail letter.

"Open it, you dope," Wilbur said.

Lincoln felt sort of frozen outside and quivery like jelly inside as he tore open the envelope and pulled out the letter. It was short. Four lines. He read: "We are pleased to advise you that you are a winner in the Hiram's Hash contest. Your prize will be delivered in a few days."

The letter was signed by the president of the company, whose name wasn't Hiram at all, but Jason Winkler, Jr.

Everyone was excited. The twins hugged him. Bunky's eyes were wide with hero worship. "From now on you're Lucky Lincoln," Wilbur said.

Success! It was sweet. It made everything different. Unreal. It seemed to Lincoln that his feet didn't touch the floor, and his head floated up around the ceiling somewhere.

Bunky ran around in circles shouting, "We've got a color TV for our clubhouse . . . we've got a color TV. . . ."

Sassy outshouted him. "What do you mean for the clubhouse? We'll use it right here at home."

"Yes," Sissy said. "Lincoln can take our old black and white set to the dugout. The picture's pretty awful anyhow."

Bunky stuck out his chin. "I own ten percent of the prize. My part goes to the clubhouse."

"What's your part?" Sassy asked.

"The aerial," Bunky said.

The argument raged, but Lincoln was above such petty squabbling. Half an hour ago he had been just plain Lincoln. Now he was Lucky Lincoln. A winner. Like a star athlete hoisted on the shoulders of his teammates. And down there below someplace was Hands and his crummy Stickball Club. He, Lucky Lincoln, would keep right on winning until he was the biggest contest star in New York City. Maybe in the whole country.

"Stop arguing," he said, from his heady elevation. "I'll probably win another color TV tomorrow. The first one goes to the clubhouse."

That silenced everyone. Lucky Lincoln, the winner, had spoken.

Lincoln's prize arrived two days later. When he came loping home from school with Wilbur, Bunky was waiting for him. "The TV is here," he cried. "It just came."

Sissy and Sassy were at the open window. "Hurry, we can hardly wait," Sassy yelled.

The boys rushed into the apartment. A big box stood in the middle of the living room. Lincoln got a knife from the kitchen and slashed it open. A notice in bold letters lay on the top. It read:

> CONGRATULATIONS
> We are sure you will be delighted with your prize in HIRAM'S HASH CONTEST: 12 dozen cans of Hiram's mouth-watering hash!

The blow stunned Lincoln speechless.

Bunky stuck his head in the box. "You mean we don't get a color TV for the clubhouse?"

Sassy took a handful of the shredded paper from around the cans, wadded it into a ring, and stuck it on Lincoln's head. "Hail, the Hash King of Plum Street."

"Cheer up," Sissy said. "It's better to have a booby prize than no prize at all."

"Aw, slice it off," Lincoln said. "So I didn't get first today. I probably will tomorrow."

Now the postman had mail for Lincoln. And packages.

Lincoln didn't win the clock-radio in the Magic Shaving Cream contest, but he did get a year's supply of shaving cream.

He didn't get the electric guitar for his name "Astrostars" in the Name the Cookie contest, but he did get a cookbook.

He missed out on the ping-pong table in the Count the Rabbits in the Cabbage Patch contest, but he won one hundred balloons. Not all blown up, of course, but deflated and neatly packed in a box.

Lincoln won a birdhouse, but he didn't have a tree to hang it in.

He lost out on the barbells in the Name the Buffalo contest, but he did win twelve skiing lessons in Idaho.

Of course, there were contests he didn't hear from, and there were contests where everyone who entered won a prize, and maybe it was something silly only a girl would want, like a tin ring with glass rubies. His room was cluttered with booby prizes. There were measuring cups and key chains, watch charms and pencil sharpeners. A kite hung from the ceiling. Cartons were under his bed and piled up against the wall. Shredded paper littered the rug.

One Saturday Sara tried to vacuum his room. She was in a bad humor, having had another tiff with Wilbur's older brother, Roscoe. "Going into your room is as dangerous as crossing Broadway at Forty-second Street," she said. "You'll just have to find some other place to put all this junk."

"Where?" Lincoln asked. "I gave Mom as much hash and soap as she could get into her cupboard. Pop said two tubes of shaving cream would last him until New Year's."

"Well, you'd better find a way to get rid of it. It's about time for Grandpa's visit, and he always shares your room."

Lincoln was still thinking about it a week later when Sara again tackled his room. This time she really blew. She banged the vacuum cleaner, knocked over a box, and began shrieking.

Mom came hurrying into Lincoln's room, all dressed up, ready to go to a meeting. She looked around; then she gave a "no fooling" order. "I want to find your room cleared out when I get back. Give these things away or take them around the corner to the junkman. Don't waste any time. He closes at noon on Saturday."

"I'll get only about one cent a pound," Lincoln wailed. But no one listened.

Lincoln looked about at all his prizes. He had got used to having them in his room. While they were around, he had some hope that the next package would be something worthwhile. Time was running out on his scheme to show up Hands. If he could only think of something.

He went outside and sat on the steps, feeling glummer than glum. Bunky came along. He had a new entry blank. It was for a canned spinach contest. "Look, Link, this is the best kind. You don't have to do a thing but write your name and address. The first prize is an automobile. Wouldn't it be neat if the Plum Street Athletic Club had its own automobile?"

"What's the booby prize, Bunk?"

"They're giving away a hundred thousand nifty can openers."

"That's just what I need, one hundred thousand can openers to get into my room," Lincoln said, handing the blank to Bunky. "Why don't you try it?"

"Me? You're the lucky one. I can't even write good."

Sara came out of the apartment with Baby Herman. She put him in his stroller. "Mom meant it about your room," she said, as she started down the street.

Meanwhile, Fats Butch was walking up the street toward the drugstore. He stopped in front of Lincoln and Bunky to scratch himself.

"He's got fleas," Bunky said.

"Yeah, he's a regular flea bag. Why, he's got so many fleas he could open a flea market . . . *Flea Market!* . . . *FLEA MARKET!*"

Lincoln jumped to his feet. "Bunky, I've got an idea. We're going to have a flea market."

"You mean we're going to hop around like fleas on a dog's back?" Bunky asked.

"No, but our customers will. You get Wilbur. Hurry. I'm calling a meeting. In my room."

6

"YOU'VE HAD SOME balmy ideas, Link," Wilbur said, threading his way through Lincoln's room. "But this flea market is the balmiest of the balmiest."

"I saw a trained flea once," Bunky said from his perch on a carton. "It was on TV, and the flea had on a shirt and cap."

"Well, it's not that kind of flea," Lincoln said.

Sassy stood in the doorway, beating a pan of fudge. "I know what you mean. It's a thing you do to get rid of stuff you don't want any more."

"You mean like a rummage sale?" Sissy asked, poking her head over Sassy's shoulder.

"Sort of," Lincoln said.

"Where you going to do all this?" Wilbur asked.

46

"I've got it all figured out," Lincoln said, looking out the window where Sara was sitting on the stoop now. "We'll load everything up, and then we'll take the long way around so Sara thinks we're headed for the junkman. Instead we'll go around the block and set up our market along the fence behind Mr. Woods' drugstore right by the gate. Lots of people pass there on the way to the supermarket. People will buy just anything at a flea market. I read that somewhere. I think I'll even sell my old comic books."

Lincoln's enthusiasm rubbed off. Now everyone wanted to get into the act.

"I'll donate this fudge," Sassy said.

"I'll make some lemon cool," Sissy said.

"If we blow up all the balloons you won, we can get a dime apiece," Wilbur said.

"Great!" Lincoln said. "I hearby make you chief balloon blower-upper. Okay now, everyone. Move."

"What's my job?" Bunky asked.

"You see that our club sign has a good spot, and you are in charge of taking a picture of the flea market."

Bunky beamed at his assignment, but then he got a worried look on his face. "How about Mr. Woods?"

"Don't worry about him. He doesn't start working until noon on Saturdays because he works Saturday night. All we have to worry about is Sara. She's going to sit there until she sees us going toward the junkman."

"I think she's sitting there hoping she'll see Roscoe," Sassy said. "She's sure grouchy when they've had a fight."

"She's got a long wait then," Wilbur said. "He's off to Coney Island."

Lincoln got his skate board and loaded a box on it. "Say, Wilbur, how about borrowing your baby sister's buggy? It will hold loads of things."

"I'll borrow it if someone else pushes it," Wilbur said.

Bunky ran home for his express wagon, and the twins loaded Mom's shopping cart.

"We'll use the clubhouse card table to display things," Lincoln said.

"Am I ever running out of breath on these balloons!" Wilbur groaned.

When all was ready, Lincoln led the procession past Sara's eagle eye, on down the street and around the subway corner. They passed the junkman and continued on around the block to the fence in the rear of Mr. Woods' drugstore.

48

The flea market took up a lot more of the sidewalk than Lincoln had figured on, so that if more than two people passed, one of them had to step off the curb into the gutter.

The card table was stacked with cans of Hiram's Hash, soap powder, et cetera, et cetera, et cetera. It held Sassy's fudge, which had not hardened — she planned to sell it by the spoonful. Sissy's lemon cool was in a bucket under the table. Lincoln tasted it and changed the sign from: FIVE CENTS A CUP to TWO FOR A NICKEL.

Bunky tacked the club sign to the fence.

Lincoln made a megaphone out of newspaper. When all was ready, he put it to his mouth: *"Hurry hurry hurry,"* he shouted.

Mrs. Ortega, who lived a few doors down from the Farnums, was their first customer. She was on her way home from morning church. She bought the cookbook for fifteen cents. "So I can cook in English," she said.

On her way to market, Mrs. Jones bought three cans of hash at ten cents a can.

Sassy acted as cashier. She kept the money in a peanut butter jar. Sissy wrapped the packages in newspaper.

"Hurry hurry hurry," Lincoln shouted.

Mrs. Krutznitt came along, carrying her cat. She handled everything on the table.

Kids from the neighborhood started coming in twos and threes and then by the dozen. They swarmed around the table. Wilbur did a brisk business in balloons. Now the kids came from every direction. They spilled out over the sidewalk into the street. They climbed the fence. They made awful faces over Sissy's lemonade and tried Sassy's fudge.

50

"*Hurry hurry hurry,*" Lincoln shouted.

This was great. He'd sell every item at this rate.

Mrs. Krutznitt was in the center of the crowd, just about ready to buy the birdhouse Lincoln had won in an ice-cream-naming contest, when her cat popped out of her arms into what was left of Sassy's fudge. The cat walked on fudge feet across the table. Mrs. Krutznitt dropped the birdhouse and lunged over the table for the cat.

At the same moment Lincoln spied three Stickballers in the crowd, and he saw a big pair of hands reach up and snip the cord holding the balloons. A gust of wind scattered them. The kids surged forward to grab them. The legs of the card table gave way. The table crashed to the sidewalk. A box of soap broke open and spilled out. Sissy's bucket of lemon cool tipped over. Soap and lemon water made a lot of suds that bubbled into the gutter.

Lincoln heard a police whistle. Kids scattered. Officer Roberts appeared. "What's going on?" he shouted.

"It's a flea market," Bunky squeaked.

"Well, it looks like a disaster area. Who's in charge?" Lincoln stepped forward.

"I'll have your peddler's license," Officer Roberts said.

Lincoln looked at him, openmouthed.

"I see," Officer Roberts said, taking a book from his pocket. "Selling without a permit, creating a public nuisance, blocking the sidewalks of New York." He looked at his wristwatch. "I'll be back in fifteen minutes, and I want this scene mopped up." He put the book away without writing in it and left.

They huddled, wondering what to do.

Lincoln knew that Officer Roberts meant what he said.

"There's the junkman," Wilbur said.

Lincoln shook his head. "It's after twelve. I could see that by Officer Roberts' wristwatch."

"I hate to mention it," Sassy said. "But half of your fifteen minutes must be gone by now. You'd better hurry and make up your mind or we'll all spend the night in jail."

Lincoln had visions of Pop coming to bail them out. Well, he surely had got himself into trouble. And one trouble led to another. He took the plunge. "We'll rush everything into the dugout until Monday, when we can take it over to the junkman's. So let's get with it."

He grabbed the birdhouse and a couple of cartons and sprinted to the cellar. When he got back to the sidewalk, Wilbur had the baby buggy piled high and was halfway through the gate. Sassy was following with the loaded-up express wagon, Sissy was cleaning the mess off the sidewalk, and Bunky was getting ready to take a picture, focusing on his sign.

Onto the scene strode stringy Mr. Woods. *"Out!"* OUT!!!" he shouted, his jaws working, his arm upraised menacingly.

53

Wilbur and Sassy pushed their cargoes through the gate and out of sight. Lincoln pulled off the sign. Sissy kept on with the mop-up. Bunky stuck the camera in his jacket, as if he thought Mr. Woods would take it from him.

Mr. Woods strode up to Lincoln, and for a moment words failed him; but when they came, they rushed out like an express train highballing it through the subway. "I gave you permission to use the space behind my building to practice basketball. For nothing else. You've made a public dump out of my property. Now off it, all of you. I don't want to see you near it again."

"But we've already put some of Lincoln's prizes in the clubhouse," Bunky said.

"Clubhouse?"

"He means the coal cellar," Lincoln said. "We didn't have any other place to store them."

"So you snooped around until you found it. And then you used it without permission," Mr. Woods said coldly, folding his arms over his chest. "Well, what's on my property belongs to me."

"You can't do that," Wilbur said. "I've got to get the baby buggy back home."

"My express wagon's in there," Bunky wailed.

Mr. Woods' smile was right off an iceberg. "It will give me great pleasure to personally see to it that all the debris you put on my property is carted to the dump. From now on, this gate is padlocked."

No one said a word on the way home. When they reached the apartment, Wilbur said, "Hands started it all. He cut the cord that held the balloons."

A tear rolled down Bunky's cheek. "He lost us our clubhouse."

Lincoln nodded. "I know."

And then he began to plot how to get even.

7

LINCOLN SAT ON THE edge of his bed, listening to a record but not really hearing it. His room was all slicked up. With the prizes gone, nothing hanging from the ceiling, nothing sticking out from under the bed, it was like an empty shell.

He felt like an empty shell, too. No brains. He'd lost the place to play basketball and any chance at having a clubhouse. The worst of it was he'd have to tell Pop what had happened because he couldn't think of any other way of getting Wilbur's mother's baby buggy and Bunky's express wagon back.

And Hands was the cause of it all.

Getting even with him wasn't that easy. How could you cut down someone who was not only bigger than you but who, sad to admit it, was also plenty smart and was surrounded by those Stickball club members of his who didn't know what a boob he was. He had to face it. Hands had everything, and he had nothing.

Disgusted, he got to his feet and went out into the living room, where Sissy and Sassy were tripping about in some of Mom's old heels.

"We're pretending we're old-time movie stars," Sissy said. "Want to play? You can be a matinee idol."

Lincoln made a face, flopped into a chair, and buried his face in a comic book.

"What you so sore about?" Sassy asked. "Just because Hands wrecked your old flea market, you don't have to be mad at everyone."

"Well, why shouldn't I be?" Lincoln asked. "Hands is the meanest, the ugliest kid I know. There isn't one good thing about him."

"I wouldn't say that," Sassy said, twirling across the room. "I think he's kind of cute."

"*Girls!*" Lincoln shouted, and he slammed out of the apartment.

He leaned against the building, thinking. He decided that even before he had his terrible revenge, he would try to get Mr. Woods to let him have the baby buggy and express wagon. He didn't think he had a chance. Mr. Woods would probably call Officer Roberts the minute Lincoln showed his face in the drugstore. But he had to try.

He started walking.

A little group of people was standing in front of the camera shop. As he got closer, he saw that Wilbur and Bunky were there. When Bunky spied him, he yelled, "Hurry, Link, look what's in the window."

Every day the new owner of the camera shop displayed the best picture of the day mounted on a large cardboard. As Lincoln got closer, he read what was printed above today's picture:

BUY AN INSTANT CAMERA AND GET INSTANT RESULTS. THIS NEWS PICTURE WAS TAKEN AN HOUR AGO.

Lincoln went closer. For golly sakes, it was a picture of the flea market.

Bunky pushed in next to Lincoln. "You told me to take a picture of the flea market, and the camera man put it in the window."

"Well, what do you know!" There was Lincoln taking down the sign, there was Wilbur pushing the baby buggy through the gate, and Sassy pulling the express wagon. Sissy was mopping up. But, best of all, there was Mr. Woods, with hand upraised, jaws open, at the very moment he was ordering them off his property. But the strange part of it was that in the picture Mr. Woods didn't look mad. He seemed to be pointing with pride to their sign: THE PLUM STREET ATHLETIC CLUB.

Apparently that's what the camera store man had thought, too, because under the picture he had printed:

MOVING DAY
PLUM STREET DRUGGIST ANGELS
ATHLETIC CLUB

Mr. Woods an angel?

It was so funny Lincoln began to laugh. He couldn't

stop. Soon Wilbur and Bunky were laughing, too. They laughed so hard everyone who passed smiled.

"Bunky, how did the picture get in the window?" Lincoln finally managed to ask.

"I gave it to the camera shop man. You told me to try a contest, and I thought maybe I'd get a prize. But you were right, he gives prizes only for pretty scenery."

Just then Mrs. Farnum and three members of the community club came by, returning from their meeting.

"Look at the picture I took, Mrs. Farnum," Bunky yelled. "It's in the window."

Mrs. Farnum went up to the window and had a look. She beckoned to her friends. They joined her.

More trouble, Lincoln thought.

Mrs. Farnum called over her shoulder. "Lincoln, please get Mr. Woods."

It was only ten steps to the drugstore, but Lincoln felt as if he were walking in wet cement. He was afraid to go inside. He stuck his head in the door, and sure enough there was Mr. Woods eyeing him, daring him to take another step. "My Mom wants to see you. She's next door," Lincoln yelled and backed away. He leaned against the drugstore window, closed his eyes, and tried to imagine what horrible fate awaited him.

When he opened them, for golly sakes, there were the
women talking excitedly, pointing to the picture in the window, and his mother was smiling, shaking hands with Mr.
Woods, and saying, "You're a great man, doing this for our
boys."

Mr. Woods was a man taken by surprise, Lincoln could
tell that. He went to the window and looked to see what
great thing he had done. He scratched his head. He got red
in the face. He coughed a couple of times. Then he stuck
out his chest and strutted a little. He began to beam. The

smile looked strange, but kind of good, on his face. "It's nothing, nothing at all," he said. "Just a little unused space I thought the boys could use."

Lincoln grinned. "Do you know what, Bunky? You just won a real big *first* prize."

"*We* won it," Bunky said. "We're partners."

Wilbur swaggered a little. "Now we've got a clubhouse, every kid on Plum Street will want to join us. Will that ever make Hands mad! Let's mosey over to his block and do some bragging."

"We'll have to yell loud and clear to beat his bragging," Lincoln said, getting into stride.

But as they went down the street, somehow it didn't seem important to Lincoln to brag. Now that they really had a clubhouse, he didn't much care to tell Hands.

He slowed up.

He stopped.

Then he clapped a hand to his forehead. "I just now tumbled. Do you know what? I think Hands has been trying to tell us something."

"What?" Bunky asked.

"That he wants to join us."

"He's got his own clubhouse," Wilbur said.